To all who have,

have had,

and will have

the SPARK.

(And to my parents, for giving me mine.)

ABOUT THIS BOOK

The illustrations for this book were done in pencil and watercolor on watercolor paper. This book was edited by Megan Tingley and Esther Cajahuaringa and designed by David Caplan and Kelly Brennan. The production was supervised by Virginia Lawther, and the production editor was Marisa Finkelstein. The text was set in Agenda, and the display type is hand-lettered.

SPARK

Ani Castillo

Megan Tingley Books
LITTLE, BROWN AND COMPANY
New York Boston

What is this magical thing…

to be alive?

Where was I
before I was born?

How many people
were born before me?

How many people have
had the spark?

And were able . . .

to touch,

to smell,

to hear,

to laugh

and tell,

to cry,

to sleep

and dream,

to make,

to dance,

to give,

to love

and share . . .

TO

How did we get so lucky
to call this universe HOME?

To be given this wonderful chance,
to be alive!

What will I do?

All on
my
own

or maybe...with YOU?

What places will we see?

Whose hearts will we touch?

Here in this world—

There's so much to be thankful for,

right here, right now.

This moment is grand!

What new adventures
will the future bring?

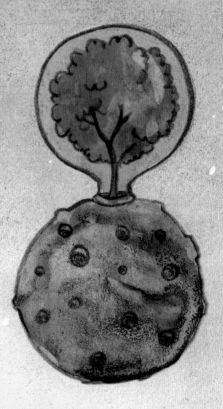

I can't wait to find out.

how freezing the snow,

or how dark the long night,

there's one thing
that's all right.

You and me, today, have this gift,
this beautiful gift.

We
have
the
SPARK!

WE ARE